TRAVELING DOWN
LIFE'S ROAD

TRAVELING DOWN LIFE'S ROAD

CURTIS BOOHER

ReadersMagnet, LLC

Traveling Down Life's Road
Copyright © 2020 by Curtis Booher

Published in the United States of America
ISBN Paperback: 978-1-950947-38-6
ISBN Hardback: 978-1-950947-98-0
ISBN eBook: 978-1-950947-39-3

All rights reserved. No part of this publication may be reproduced, stored in a retrieval system or transmitted in any way by any means, electronic, mechanical, photocopy, recording or otherwise without the prior permission of the author except as provided by USA copyright law.

The opinions expressed by the author are not necessarily those of ReadersMagnet, LLC.

ReadersMagnet, LLC
10620 Treena Street, Suite 230 | San Diego, California, 92131 USA
1.619. 354. 2643 | www.readersmagnet.com

Book design copyright © 2020 by ReadersMagnet, LLC. All rights reserved.
Cover design by Ericka Walker
Interior design by Shemaryl Evans
Illustrated by Jebb

DEDICATION

This book is dedicated in memory of my parents
Roy and Eunice Booher.

ACKNOWLEDGMENT

Curtis Booher loves the Lord and he loves to express that love through poetry. You will clearly see that as you read these poems. Curtis was born and reared in central Oklahoma. My acquaintance with him goes back some 40 years. I know him to be an avid sports fan both as a player on the field and as a very knowledgeable spectator and analyzer of various sporting events.

More importantly, however, is the fact that Curtis is a sincerely committed Christian man. Through his poems in this book he presents the Gospel message in all its beauty and power. He exalts God as the awesome and powerful creator. He emphasizes Christ, the cross, and the blood of Christ as the means of our cleansing from sin. Not to be missed is his emphasis on the heavenly home for all who accept and follow Christ. These themes are presented over and over again in many unique ways.

Several of these poems were used by Curtis as communion meditations or as inspirational readings in a church I served where he was a member. They were always appreciated, I recommend these poems as a refreshing read. They speak to that which we all as Christians have felt at times. They will be a clear reminder of God's grace and love for us through his son Jesus Christ. And by the way, don't miss the poems entitled, "Mother" and "My Dad, My Father."

Howard Faerber
Christian Minister

CONTENTS

1	My Father Owns the Thunder	1
2	I Can't Wait to See His Face	3
3	One Day Closer to Home	4
4	Just Beyond the Storm	5
5	Dance in the Clouds	6
6	Life's Road	8
7	All Better	9
8	Where All the Children Play	10
9	Never Further Than His Name	11
10	Pass It 'Round	14
11	My Sack of Sins	15
12	Two Trees	17
13	A Place to Wait	18
14	The Master Architect	19
15	Mother	21
16	A Song in the Night	23
17	A Rich and Fertile Land	24
18	I Am the Reason	25

19	Found	26
20	Christmas Together	27
21	In Remembrance of Him	29
22	What a Way to Go	30
23	Prime Property	31
24	My Dad, My Father	33
25	Candle Holder	34
26	The Pathway	35
27	Footprints in the Snow	36
28	The Master's Great Bouquet	37
29	My Promise	38
30	The Old Vessel	39
31	With Me	41
32	Road to Nowhere	42
33	Can You Save Me	43
34	Forgotten	45
35	My Name	46
36	Salvation Cruise	47
37	Death	48
38	Earth	49
39	It's Christmas	51
40	Highway of Holiness	52
41	It Was Love	53

42	Keys	54
43	Running with the Wind	55
44	The Sea of Forgetfulness	56
45	My Ragged Old Tent	57
46	The Man from the Box	58
47	He Left the Light On	60
48	What Would Have Been	61
49	Lean on the Cross	62
50	Water on the Rocks	64
51	The Advocate	65
52	No Time	67
53	He Borrowed a Donkey	69
54	Red Carpet	71
55	My Guardian	73
56	The Book That Says It All	74
57	Three Rusty Nails	75
58	The Steward	76
59	A Hammer and Those Nails	77
60	Guilty	78
61	The Pitcher	79
62	God's Greatness	80
63	With Both Hands	81
64	The Man from the Shore	82

65	Today	84
66	Exit Signs	85
67	All Outdoors	86
68	King of the Hill	87
69	In the Twinkling of an Eye	88
70	My Friend	89

MY FATHER OWNS THE THUNDER

As the rich man gave a cup of soup to the hobo, he did say,
"I will earn my way to heaven by giving you soup today.
And I know not why God made me a better man than you,
or why it is that heaven waits for just a chosen few."
The hobo quickly took the soup, then slowly raised his eyes,
and through missing teeth and bearded lips, to the rich man, he replied,
"Sir, I truly thank you for this meal you've given me,
but there are things about heaven, sir, I'm afraid you do not see.
Sir, heaven is not a place you earn, you get there through God's grace,
no matter what your wealth is or the color of your face.
And if a man's value to you is just in what he owns,
and you think that rich includes a big ole fancy home,
then, sir, it will impress you that I have a mansion to behold,
a mansion my father's given me, it's built on streets of gold.

My Father Owns the Thunder, the lightning, and the rain,
He owns every foot of land from Russia around to Spain.
I am a wealthy Christian in spirit and in soul,
I have an inheritance waiting for me that "ole Tut's tomb can't hold."
As the hobo soaked some dried out bread in his cup of soup,
he said, "That's a pretty golden chain in the vest of your silk suit.
I see you wearing diamond rings and gold upon your hands,
Sir, they can be used for collateral here, but not in the promised land.
Don't put your trust in worldly things for they will rust and fade away,

put your trust in Jesus, before it is too late.
Then you can own true riches like the wind and the gentle breeze,
just by falling on your knees, and saying, Jesus, forgive me please.
Then when Satan comes soul shopping on that judgment day,
you cannot afford me, you can boldly say.

My Father Owns the Thunder, the lightning, and the rain,
He owns every foot of land from Russia around to Spain.
I am a wealthy Christian in spirit and in soul,
And I have an inheritance waiting for me that ole Tut's tomb can't hold.
My Father Owns the Thunder, the lightning, and the rain,
He owns all the oil flowing through earth's veins.
My Father Owns the Thunder, the lightning, and the rain,
He owns all the lumber, all the minerals, wheat, and grain.
My Father Owns the Thunder, the lightning, and the rain,
He owns all the livestock grazing on the plains.

My Father Owns the Thunder!"

I CAN'T WAIT TO SEE HIS FACE

If God's beauty is seen in an evening sunset,
or seen from a mountain where the view takes your breath.
Or if His beauty is seen in river rapids that race,
then I Can't Wait to See His Face.

If God's beauty is seen in fields of golden ripe grain,
or seen in a rainbow, right after a rain.
Or if it's seen as an eagle that soars with power and grace,
then I Can't Wait to See His Face.

If God's beauty is seen in vast oceans of blue,
or seen as a rose freshly kissed by the dew.
Or if it's seen in a brilliant sunrise at the start of the day,
then I Can't Wait to See His Face.

No, I cannot imagine all the beauty that waits,
when I set foot in heaven 'neath those bright pearly gates.
And I can't imagine all the beauty I'll see,
when I see the one that paints each autumn leaf.
Oh! I can hardly wait to see that radiant place,
where all the beauty is a reflection of my sweet savior's face.

ONE DAY CLOSER TO HOME

One Day Closer to Home, we're One Day Closer to Home,
see the lights of the city, we're One Day Closer to Home.
Soon we will cross that river and rest in a peaceful land,
we will dine with the master and touch His nail-scarred hands.

We will Hear the angels singing, as we near the pearly gates,
see the lights of the city, I can hardly wait.
We will visit with old loved ones, who have already made it home,
there we will stay forever, no more must we roam.

Soon we will walk on streets of gold, as we take that heavenly tour,
we will find the journey has well been worth, every hardship we've endured.
This old body will be young and strong, when healing hands touch me,
deaf ears will hear the singing, and all blind eyes shall see.

Gabriel now stands ready, to make that trumpet sound,
the journey is almost over, we are homeward bound.
One Day Closer to Home, One Day Closer to Home,
the journey is almost over, we are One Day Closer to Home.

JUST BEYOND THE STORM

As thunderstorms rumbled in the night, and lightning walked the sky,
as a child I'd become afraid, because storms would make me cry.
But Dad would put an arm 'round me, and in a voice kind and warm,
would say, "Son, don't worry about each and every storm.
For life will have its rainy days, but each storm will pass on through,
and beyond each storm is a peace and calm and skies of powder blue."
But too soon, life's storms took their toll, and we lost Dad one day,
that's when I thought that Mama would be the one afraid.
But as I held her precious hand, she smiled so soft and warm,
saying, "Your daddy's reached that peace and calm, Just Beyond the Storm."

Now there's no thunder overhead, no lightning in the sky,
and though time has passed and I'm a man,
I'm in a storm that makes me cry.
For in that limousine up ahead, that soft smile on her face,
Mama makes that journey to her final resting place.
But then my tears are put aside, by a feeling oh so warm,
I know Mom and Dad are walking hand in hand, just beyond the storm.

Now storms will come and storms will go, but no storm will ever last,
and though life's clouds hang overhead, they too will surely pass.
So when thunder rumbles 'round us and dark clouds begin to form,
Rest assured there's peace and calm, Just Beyond the Storm.

DANCE IN THE CLOUDS

Whether my eyes are closed or my head is bowed,
I can see your beautiful face as you Dance in the Clouds.
At night as stars shine overhead and their beauty lights the sky,
I am reminded of the happiness I saw in you sparkling eyes.
When I feel a gentle breeze softly touch my skin,
it is as though your soft hair is brushing against me once again.
In a hypnotic trance through a distant stare,
in my mind as clouds swirl in the sky, I see you dancing there.

Oh, how I'd love to kiss you and taste your soft warm lips,
and once again hold and caress you with my fingertips.
With so much love left here unused,
we will have that much more to share when I get there with you.
If I could take hold of your hand by simply reaching out,
I would step from here to there and join you in the clouds.
One day I will leave this lonely world in that there is no doubt,
then forever hand in hand together, we will Dance in the Clouds.

LIFE'S ROAD

Life's Road is there to challenge me each morning when I rise,
with dips and valleys, twist and turns, and hills that reach the skies.
Sometimes the road runs straight and smooth, with no obstacles insight,
but suddenly, it can change, and I need all my strength to climb.

Life's Road continues on, through the sunshine and the storms,
sometimes there is no shelter or a place where I can warm.
The view at times is beautiful, with sights that take my breath away,
then times the sights are not as nice and make the bold afraid.

Life's Road has peaks and valleys, and cross roads that lead astray,
slippery slopes and dark alleys that cause me to lose my way.
Dangerous curves may lie ahead, with no warning signs in sight,
making it so very easy to run off the road of life.

A guide was sent from heaven above to lead me every day,
and thru all the twist and turns that remain, He'll gladly show the way.
He lifts me up when I am down, He'll bear my heavy load,
I just hold on to his nail-scarred hand, and let Him lead me down Life's Road.

ALL BETTER

She would play out in the sunshine, sometimes too recklessly,
for she might fall and scratch her arm or maybe bruise her knee.
But her mother was always close enough to wipe away the tears,
her mother was her savior, throughout her childhood years.
For if the hurt were big or small, it didn't really matter,
her mother's touch and soft warm kiss would make the hurt All Better.

But after years of watching sunsets, pain came that would not cease,
and it seemed to use up all her strength, just to try to breath.
Her children learned at an early age that she had her mother's touch,
and their children too would run to her, with a bruise that they would clutch.
For if the hurt were big or small, it really didn't matter,
her special touch and soft warm kiss would make the hurt All Better.

Now she has moved beyond the sunset, where pain is in the past,
where there is neither crutch or cough nor lame that cannot move fast.
She can walk and run forever without each breath requiring labor,
for she now walks on streets of gold, with Jesus Christ,
her lord and savior,
Where if your hurt is big or small, it really doesn't matter;
His special touch and soft warm kiss will heal the hurt forever.

WHERE ALL THE CHILDREN PLAY

The other day as I was driving down a busy street,
a man lay on the sidewalk, a whiskey bottle at his feet.
I thought this world is cruel, it can twist a man so tight,
it wraps itself around you until it eats all your mind.
Then I saw a little girl with braces on her legs,
sitting outside a busy playground, as she watched the other children play,
I thought this world is cruel, there must be a peaceful place,
where minds are not tormented and all the children play.
That night as I lay sleeping in my deepest dreams,
I dreamed I received a letter that was addressed just to me.
In the left hand corner where the sender's name is placed,
it simply said, "Jesus, Where All the Children Play."
When I opened up the letter to see just what it said,
I could tell a blood-stained nail was used to write these words in red.
It said, "The world is cruel, so I prepared a peaceful place,
where minds are not tormented, and all the children play."
The letter read, "The world is so cruel, it crucified the perfect man,
but I love the world so much, I came and died for every man.
Up here there is no sickness, no sorrow, just joy on every face."
The letter was signed, Love, Jesus, Where All the Children Play.

NEVER FURTHER THAN HIS NAME

As I looked into the sky, oh! how I wished that I could fly,
for heaven seemed so very far away.
Without wings, I couldn't try, and it made me want to cry,
knowing in this old world I would have to stay.
I wondered if somewhere, there might be a flight of stairs,
that would take me right up to heaven's door.
I was now deep in despair, thinking no one really cared,
that I would burn in hell for evermore.

Though it looked so very far, I had to get up past the stars,
for it looked to be such a peaceful place.
If someone would tell how, I would leave for there right now,
even if it meant I'd have to pay.
I thought there just had to be a way to escape this sinful place,
and here, I did not want to spend eternity.
I knew an answer lay somewhere on how to get from here to there,
so I would search the world over, from sea to shining sea.

Then a bearded man got my attention, so I quickly stopped and listened
as he spoke on a street corner in a busy town.
I saw hope there in his eyes, as he held a cardboard sign
that read, "Find Jesus, it's through Him that heaven can be found."
I said, "This Jesus on your sign, is He very hard to find?
For on my own I just cannot find the way."

He answered, "He's not hard to find at all, if on His name you will simply call, and He will meet you anytime, anyplace.

But if you think that you must search, across the street is an old church, and I'm sure that you can find Him waiting there."
I quickly reached into my pocket, pulled out a golden locket
and asked, "Do you think this will be enough to pay the fare?"
The man said, "He will take you there Himself no matter what your wealth,
for Jesus came to save the lost.
Jesus came here for you and to give you life anew,
and for you to get to heaven, He has already paid the cost."

I asked, "What's the color of His eyes, how can He be recognized,
you see I've never met the man before."
He said, "You will know Him when you meet, by scars, on His hands and feet and scars left by a crown of thorns."
I kept my eye on that church steeple, as I shoved my way between the people,
and began to dodge the traffic in the lanes.
Above the crowd and all the noise, again I heard the bearded man's voice
as he shouted out, "Find Jesus, you are the reason that He came."

Oh, how I was hoping, as I yanked those church doors open,
that I would find Jesus waiting just inside.
But my heart fell to the ground, for there was no one else around,
and I was so sad, I felt I'd die.
I thought I had sealed my eternal fate by arriving here too late,
for Jesus was no longer here.
With my last chance for heaven faltered, I fell down on an old altar,
and began to cry heartbroken tears.

There on bended knees, I whispered, "Jesus, save me please,

for without you, all hope for me is gone."

Then the heaven I'd been searching for met me right there on the floor,

as I heard angels sing a joyful song.

As I stood upon my feet, again I heard the bearded man out in the street

shouting, "Find Jesus, you are the reason that He came."

Now I can truly say, "Heaven is not that far away,

for heaven is Never Further Than His Name."

PASS IT 'ROUND

On the table sets a pan of steaming biscuits, fluffy, soft, and brown,
help yourself to the biscuits, then pass the biscuits 'round.
There's churned butter on the table, at least half a pound,
help yourself to the butter, then pass the butter 'round.

If you'd like some honey, squeeze the honey bear upside down,
help yourself to the honey, then pass the honey 'round.
That was my mama's breakfast table, in a small quiet country town,
we took some of everything, then we'd Pass It 'Round.

Now God's prepared for us a table, with much more than we deserve,
so pull up a chair and have a seat, He is waiting anxiously to serve.
His table is covered with a beautiful blood-red tablecloth,
and for all that we receive, He has paid the cost.

Forgiveness is abundantly placed at our fingertips,
God knew we'd need a lot of it and be making several trips.
God's goodness is always fresh, it never has to be thrown out,
things never seen on His table are hate, anger, fear, and doubt.

On our plate is the lamb of God, and salvation, enough to last an eternity,
it's a mystery, why He would serve such a delicacy, to a sinner such as me.
Grace and love come by the basket full, God's table just abounds,
take all you want of everything, then kindly Pass It 'Round.

MY SACK OF SINS

The road was smooth when my trip began,
and with no weight on my back, I sometimes ran.
But then I came to a temptation, I could not resist,
it was a small temptation, so I carried it in my fist.
Then another appeared in my path, with no way for me to dodge it,
but with plenty of room to spare, I simply carried that one in my pocket.
With every step I took, it seemed a sin was waiting there,
until my pockets were all filled up with no room to spare.

As my journey grew longer, I had sins to burn,
but I found a sack to carry them in, so I wasn't the least little bit concerned.
The road had now became rough and rugged with no turning back,
and I now had gathered so many sins they were filling up my sack.
I had been collecting sins as if they were stones,
and their weight had become too much for me to carry all alone.
I was now weak and bent from the load of sins in my sack,
they were now like a great anvil, strapped upon my back.

The road I was walking had now became very steep,
and the weight from My Sack of Sins made me fall down on my knees.
After l knelt there for a moment, tired and dirty, weary and lost,
as I wiped the sweat from my brow, I realized I had fallen at the foot of a cross.
Then a man with scarred hands reached down and lifted me up,
but the weight of my sins still caused me to slump.

He said, "I have been waiting right here watching you try walking alone, and if you will let me, for the rest of your journey, I would like to carry your load."

I was now walking straight and upright,
With my newfound friend, carrying My Sack of Sins, there by my side.
He said, "The Road I walk is a much straighter road,
I've shown many others the way and carried their load."
We walked together a long, long way, with Him bearing the weight of my sins,
and I knew I had met a true caring eternal friend.
Then He turned and said, "Continue on to your mansion brand-new,
I must go now and meet another at that old rugged cross where I met you."

TWO TREES

Two Trees were planted side by side,
there by the brook of life;
One knew it needed to drink from the brook,
on Sundays, and every Wednesday night.

The other tree thought it could keep its strength,
by just drinking now and then;
While one tree stood straight and strong against each storm,
the other kept growing weaker, as it bent beneath the wind.

The brook was there to feed both the trees,
so each could have abundant life;
While one tree bore a delicious fruit for any passerby,
the other's fruit grew bitter, as it began to dry.

Two Trees were planted side by side,
there by the brook of life;
While one kept drinking from the brook and gained eternal life,
the other gradually quit drinking from the brook,
and stood by the brook and died.

A PLACE TO WAIT

Grave, I do not fear you though you are cold and deep,
I think of you as A Place to Wait, until God calls me from death's sleep.
It has been a long and tiring trip with some rough and rugged miles,
and you will be a peaceful place to rest for just a little while.
When Gabriel blows his trumpet and makes that glorious sound,
I will awaken from my sleep, and I'll be homeward bound.
Grave, I won't be staying long, maybe just a day,
for Jesus could be coming anytime to take His bride away.
I'll be waiting here for Jesus, and I'm sure He is coming soon,
the same Jesus who defeated death by walking from a cold
and lonely tomb.
To leave this world behind me is one step closer home,
where death and graves are in the past and sorrow is unknown.
With my name chiseled in granite, you look like a permanent place,
But, grave, I do not fear you, for you are just A Place to Wait.

THE MASTER ARCHITECT

As we tour the neighborhood, keep one thing in mind,
all the structures may not please you, but one might catch your eye.
The same architect created them, each and every one,
some are already finished, while others are not completely done.
He gave them all their own free will, and they come in different frames,
to construct and resurrect them is why the architect came.
Notice the different colors that the architect may use,
to Him, color is of no consequence, though it may be to me and you.

He is the Master Architect, with a unique plan,
for He can build a temple here, then move it to a distant land.
A land where He built a city, whose dimensions are four square,
and in the twinkling of an eye, He can move a temple from here to there.
He built that city He came from, out of silver, jasper, and gold,
on the banks of a beautiful river where peaceful waters flow.
But here the structure I want to show you has a story all its own,
for though it looked to be lived in, it stood empty all alone.

The one who dwelt there did not want the architect to stay,
and soon the storms of life took their toll, when the architect was sent away.
Its insides became a filthy mess, for it was cluttered up with trash,
light could never shine inside, its shades were tightly drawn and lashed.
Pretty flowers never grew there, for weeds grew all around,

and the shutters hung from the windows, as if tears were falling down.
Then the one who dwelt there asked the architect to return,
fearing the structure he had ruined was no longer of the architect's concern.

But the architect did hurry back and embraced the ugly sight,
His tools were never put away, as He worked both day and night.
He took down the shades and let the sun light in,
soon beautiful flowers began to grow, where only weeds had been.
The architect anchored the structure to the rock of life,
now it doesn't sway to and fro, when life's storms blow, with all their might.
He rebuilt the old structure with pure and undying love,
and all the filth and trash inside were cleansed with His precious blood.

Some said, "Tear the old shack down, it's an eyesore to the neighborhood,"
but the scarred and skilled hands of the architect has it looking really good.
To let a structure perish is not the architect's will,
for with hammer and nails, He began saving them years ago, on Golgotha hill.
Why He would leave His beautiful city is a mystery no one can understand, to come and pour His life into each structure, until blood runs from His hands.
When the job was completed, on the rundown wreck,
He hung a shingle on it that reads, "It is finished!" Signed the Master Architect.

MOTHER

She may not have been perfect, although I thought she was,
even when I was a child asking "why," and she would answer, "Just because."
Her love could never be measured by any depth or height,
she brought me up to know the Lord and tried to raise me right.
I know I would have never made it, through my childhood days,
if Mother hadn't been there to help me in so many different ways.
No matter what I put her through, not once did her love cease,
whether I was good or bad or tried to go to bed with dirty hands and feet.

She knew when to build me up and when to bring me down a notch,
all the countless things she did for me kept her going 'round the clock.
Mother loved me with all her heart, in that there is no doubt,
even when I'd hear her say, "I brought you in this world, and I can take you out."
She was my cook and seamstress, my doctor and my nurse,
though I could never figure out, if the merthiolate or the cut hurt worse.
If I tore my clothes, a patch she could quickly stitch,
or if my manners needed fixing, she could just as quickly get a switch.

She was the world's greatest Mother, but I felt I was dealt a terrible fate,
when told you're not going anywhere, until you eat all that's on your plate.
If I could turn the clock back, so I could hear her say once more,
"Quit running through the house, and, child, please don't slam the door."
Whether it was taking me to church or taking me over her knee,

when she left this world, she left many precious memories.
For I can still see her in an apron, by the stove there in the kitchen,
laughing and talking, as she fixed the world's best fried chicken.

She got up early every day and went to work, so she could make ends meet,
came back home without complaint, and be right back on her feet.
I never thought about it then, I just thought that's what mothers did,
but if she ever got discouraged, she knew how to keep it hid.
No matter if it were in the yard or sitting on the porch,
how I wish I could hold her hand and say, "I love you," just once more.
If God let me do it all over again, I would never choose another,
because I know for me, He gave me, the perfect Mother.

A SONG IN THE NIGHT

With lonely darkness all around, and my spirit broken down;
when there doesn't seem to be a ray of light at all.
Through the darkness God sends a song, that lets me know that I belong
to someone who cares that my tear drops fall.

God sends a Song in the Night, that brings a brilliant ray of light;
a light that causes the darkness to roll away.
His peaceful song brings me cheer, a song that tells me not to fear,
for in my darkest hour, near me, He will always stay.

When clouds of pain are all that's found, with heavy burdens all around;
His song penetrates the darkness, as a shining light.
Just when I think my prayers have failed, and total darkness has prevailed,
God sends a Song in the Night.

A RICH AND FERTILE LAND

He pulled the reins and stopped his mule and leaned against his plow,
then from his pocket pulled a handkerchief and wiped his sweaty brow.
He raised his hand to shield his eyes, as he looked into the sun,
then whispered a prayer to the cloudless sky, for rain that would not come.

The field was plowed and ready for seed, but his crops had failed before,
like him the land was overworked, and like him, it was also poor.
As he looked back at the earth he'd turned, dust blew against his face,
dust driven by a hot angry wind, as though it were sent from hell, with rage.

Again, he wiped away the sweat, with a hard and calloused hand,
as he looked beyond the red hot sun, and dreamed of a Rich and Fertile Land.

He walked his mule back to the barn and swung open a wooden gate,
then took a dipper of cool water from a pail, as he rested on a bale of hay.
His shirt was soaked, and his back ached, as he breathed dry and lifeless air;
and from beneath his hat, sweat trickled down through grey and thinning hair.

As he looked down between his feet at the loose hay on the hard dirt floor,
he thought things were good, when she was here, wishing she were once more.
Then he thought of her gentle smile, that to him was as soft as a cool breeze,
and instead of hearing the hot wind blow, he thought he could hear angels sing.

He dreamed of being there with her, so they could go walking hand in hand,
through beautiful fields of golden wheat, in a Rich and Fertile Land.

I AM THE REASON

I am like a small pebble on the floor of the sea,
and I'm just a speck, when I stand beside a great redwood tree.
When in the Grand Canyon, I feel tiny and small,
as I stand at the bottom and look up at its towering walls.
From snowcapped mountains to huge waterfalls,
with great love and care, God created it all.
But beside these great things, I loom large in His eyes,
 I Am the Reason, He came and died.

I am like a small leaf in a hurricane's wind,
compared to a universe, to which there's no end.
In all His creations I'm so very small,
but if I simply whisper, He hears my call.
God made the oceans, the clouds in the sky,
He made the sun so the world could have light.
God hung the moon and the stars and all the planets on high,
but, I Am the Reason, He came and died.

FOUND

He walked His whole life searching for me,
behind each bush and beneath every tree.
He loved me so much He left no stone unturned,
for my Salvation was His only concern.

But where sin did abound,
that's where I would hide, so not to be Found.
In the darkness of sin, I would be safe,
for there He would never see my face.

Then, as I sat on a stone on a mountain high,
I saw what I meant to Him, as I looked Him in the eyes.
His whole life He had searched for me relentlessly.
then I Found Him, as I watched Soldiers nail Him to a tree.

CHRISTMAS TOGETHER

The sun was brightly shining on that Christmas morn,
as Mother and Dad spent Christmas together where they never had before.
This was their first Christmas Together, of so many they would spend,
with all of their old loved ones and many, many friends.

Dad had waited patiently for the woman of his dreams,
and now their spending Christmas Together, caused all the angels to sing.
We kids were now just passing thoughts, barely on their minds,
for it was much too soon yet, for any of us to arrive.

With Mama holding Daddy's hand, so proudly at his side,
I'm sure Dad's heart was pounding, and his chest filled up with pride.
The dirt road that ran by Dad's house was now paved with purest gold,
and it took them not to an old framed house, but a mansion to behold.

Now Dad could take Mom around and show her all the sights to see,
and they could take all the time they wanted since they had all eternity.
Dad was elated that Mother was there to enjoy God's eternal gift forever,
that made this Christmas very special, their first Christmas in heaven together.

IN REMEMBRANCE OF HIM

We break the bread and drink the cup In Remembrance of Him,

The perfect son God sacrificed, for our each and every sin.

He showed His love as He healed the sick, and gave sight unto the blind;

but the greatest way He showed His love for us, He came and gave His life.

For a dark and sinful world, at Golgotha He was killed,

He died that day on a cross, because it was His father's will.

He rose from the tomb in victory and is alive once again,

So we break the bread and drink the cup, In Remembrance of Him.

WHAT A WAY TO GO

Now when I breathe my final breath there will be no need for tears,
for though you may not see it, an angel will be standing near.
Then if you listen closely, you may hear a fluttering sound;
that would be the angel's wings, as we head homeward bound.
What a Way to Go, What a Way to Go,
I'm leaving here on an angel's wings, What a Way to Go.

I really am afraid of heights and I don't like to fly,
but I will have myself a first-class trip to my heavenly home on high.
We will soar right by that sweet chariot as it comes down swinging low,
and our wind will fill the sails on that old gospel ship as it picks up another load,
What a Way to Go, What a Way to Go,
I'm leaving here on an angel's wings, What a Way to Go.

I am sure we will leave a vapor trail as my angel takes me home,
we will zoom past Mars and Jupiter and stars that are unknown.
My angel will set me down on a big soft cloud right by those pearly gates,
and I can already hear Saint Peter say, "You're the first one here today."
What a Way to Go, What a Way to Go,
I'm leaving here on an angel's wings, What a Way to Go.

PRIME PROPERTY

The moment I was born, my father gave to me,
a very valuable piece of Prime Property.
It was clean and pure and untouched by man,
ready to be filled with ideas, hopes, and dreams ever so grand.
My property had an endless range, to go wherever I chose,
no walls or barriers stood in my way, I could go fast, or I could go slow.
My property reached from the bottom of the sea, to beyond the stars above;
it could soar high with eagles, and still be as gentle as a snow-white dove.
At first I was very protective of my valuable Prime Property,
and very careful not to let trespassers come near my vicinity,
But then one day, a stranger came and knocked upon my door,
offering me worldly riches and beautiful things I'd never seen before.
All he asked in return seemed like a real fair deal to me,
he just wanted to live on the very edge of my Prime Property.

So we drew up a deal, on which we both agreed,
and willingly to my property I handed him a deed.
He wasted not a minute before he started moving in,
and I was sure I had found myself a true and loyal friend.
But soon, I found he wasn't content just to stay on the edge of my property,
as he kept offering more and more of those worldly things to me.
Gradually, one step at a time, he kept moving further in,
until he was now living where no one before had ever been.
He was now living in the middle of my Prime Property,

with trash and clutter being strung about, as far as you could see.
At first I ask him kindly, if he would be nice enough to leave,
when I begged and pleaded, he simply laughed and showed to me the deed.
I had not talked to my Father about the stranger living on my property,
and the longer I waited, the more angry I knew that He would be.

The stranger kept getting bolder, until my pleading he would mock.
Finally I said, "Father, it's been a long time, but now we must have a talk."
I said, "Father, please forgive me, for all that I have done,
I have been unfaithful to you, I am not a deserving son.
I have let a stranger occupy much of my Prime Property,
and no matter what I try or say, he simply will not leave."
My Father answered, "I've known for some time a stranger was living there,
and though the property is great and vast, I do not want to share.
If you truly want him to leave, mention my name, a cross,
and mount Calvary,
and I promise you, my son, you can quickly reclaim your Prime Property."
So boldly, I confronted the evil stranger, and did what my Father had said,
soon I felt like a brand-new man, as he tore up the deed and fled.
From time to time, the wicked stranger still comes by,
to try new deals on me, but I just speak my Father's name,
and quickly he will flee.

MY DAD, MY FATHER

My Dad taught me how to throw a ball and how to bait a hook,
I recognized his voice when he spoke, I didn't have to turn around and look.
He never raised his voice when he tried to teach me wrong from right,
but he never showed much sympathy, if I came home with a shiner on my eye.

Somehow I think he meant it, when he had to take me down a notch or two,
when he said, "This is going to hurt me, son, much more than it is you."
He told me countless stories, as he sat and whittled out there on our porch,
and the love I carry for my Dad, still burns like a flaming torch.

My Father gave me the ability to throw a ball and created fish for me to hook,
though I've never heard His voice, I will recognize it, I won't need to turn and look.
He has helped me up countless times when I've slipped a notch or two,
if He were not always there for me, I don't know just what I'd do.

When He came and saved me by dying for my sins,
it really didn't hurt me, like I know that it hurt Him.
He knew He would be spit upon, nailed to a cross then,
with a spear be gorged,
but the love my Father has for me, and still burns like a flaming torch.

CANDLE HOLDER

A light was given unto me, to keep me from the dark,
a light that keeps on shining, here inside my heart.

The light is like a candle, whose flame is tall and bright,
a flame that always lights the way, in both the day and night.

Though life's winds blow very hard, the flame does not go out,
in fact, the candle burns the brightest, when the winds cause me to doubt.

The candle puts out a light, with such a glowing ray,
that I can always find the path, when I begin to lose my way.

In darkness when fear comes over me, its reflection makes me bolder,
and for that I am forever thankful, God chose me, to be a Candle Holder.

THE PATHWAY

I'm walking, yes, I'm walking with my Savior,
I'm walking, yes, I'm walking with my Lord.
He is showing me the Pathway up to glory,
the Pathway that He made for you and me.

The Pathway takes us right beside a manger,
the sight of the holy virgin birth;
God's gift from above, God's greatest gift of love,
to every lost sinner here on earth.

The Pathway now leads up Mount Calvary,
and here I see an old rugged cross.
With a crown of thorns upon His head, crucified like prophets said,
Jesus died, that no soul should be lost.

The Pathway now winds through a garden,
and here I'm shown a dark empty tomb.
From the dead Christ rose again, to deliver us from sin,
and He'll return for His church someday soon.

The Pathway now leads on up to glory,
and turns into a street of purest gold.
By God's amazing grace, He has prepared for us a place,
the street is lined with mansions to behold.

I'm walking, yes I'm walking with my Savior,
I'm walking, yes I'm walking with my Lord.
He has shown me The Pathway up to glory,
it's The Pathway that He made for you and me.

FOOTPRINTS IN THE SNOW

I try to look ahead, but I can't keep from looking back,
and all I see is my companion whenever I do that.
I see places where we laughed and places where we cried.
Every time I turn and look, I see my companion by my side.
I see a pretty meadow where we walked hand in hand,
and I see a dry riverbed with two sets of footprints in the sand.
I see a smiling face that could brighten the darkest day,
and I see my companion there beside me to help me find my way.

Now, I'm not certain I can make the journey on my own,
for in numbness I read my companion's name, chiseled there in stone.
Though I feel lost, empty, and weak, a sweet spirit tells me continue on,
for I left you with many loving memories, enough to keep you strong.
We walked this life together at one another's side,
leaving two sets of footprints, whether the path were wet or dry.
Now through tear-filled eyes the harsh reality I see,
I know my companion will no longer laugh and walk with me.
As I leave this peaceful place it is clear I walk alone,
For when I turn for one last look, I see only one set of Footprints in the Snow.

THE MASTER'S GREAT BOUQUET

As the master surveyed His garden, He held a bouquet in one hand,
but He was still in need of a flower, one, that was so very grand.
The flowers the master held were each very pretty on their own,
but He was searching for a special one that would accent His bouquet;
 and give it beauty to behold.

Then as He stopped before us, as a rare flower caught His eye,
one so nearly perfect, that it made the master sigh.
When those around were burdened, she would not hesitate to pray,
and everyone who met her knew she was destined to be in
 The Master's Great Bouquet.

She was always quick to comfort us, and there to see us through,
never once did she sway, when life's bitter winds blew.
She had a strength and inner beauty that helped the other flowers grow,
we would have been just another garden, if not for her radiant glow.

As the master's arm reached past me, it brushed away some dew,
as His scarred hand lifted up this precious sister, the one so very true.
Now, I feel so very blessed and honored, for I can truly say, I grew in the very garden, beside the beautiful flower that accents,
 The Master's Great Bouquet.

MY PROMISE

I've tried to walk the straight and narrow, and I have failed time and again;
for no matter how hard I try, I keep giving into sin.
Seems I take two steps backward before I take one ahead,
though it is made with good intentions My Promise is just empty words instead.
God is always quick to forgive and He forgives me once more,
so I make Him the same promise I've tried to keep so many times before,
After each and every failure, the one thing that I have learned.
is that God is always true to His word and gives me more love than I deserve.
Now, the only promise I will make and know it is a promise I can keep,
is the promise to continue to strive for the perfection that I seek.

THE OLD VESSEL

How much longer the Master would use it was really hard to tell,
but The Old Vessel had to wonder, as it set there by the well.
For years the master would fill it right up to the top,
and it could carry all the water to the garden and never spill a drop.
But time had now passed it by, as age began to take its toll,
and The Old Vessel could no longer do its part to help the garden grow.

The Old Vessel knew it could be put away, now at any time,
since a new stout Vessel, was now setting by its side.
The Old Vessel could not look forward to tomorrow,
today might be it's last,
for it had so many cracks now, it spilled all its water along the cobbled path.
Perhaps the Master would fill it with dirt to put a bouquet in,
or maybe stuff it full of straw, to make a nest, for a sparrow or a wren.

The Master would always fill the new stout vessel first;
then The Old Vessel would quickly be filled, and carried to the garden,
where thirsty seeds, waited in the earth.
No matter how hard It tried, too many cracks would let its water all run out;
so when they reached the garden, there was nothing left
to pour from its broken spout.

One day The Old Vessel would be carried in the Master's left hand,
the next day in His right;

as the Master carried water to a garden that the sun had surely dried.
The Old Vessel had all but given up, since it was no longer of good use,
when it heard footsteps on the cobbled path, as the Master came into view.
The morning was so beautiful, as the birds began to sing,
the flowers should be blooming soon, for it was getting late in spring.

Since The Old Vessel could no longer hold the cool water,
and could no longer do it's share;
it knew it's half the garden would be sun baked, dry, and bare.
But as they went back to the garden, The Old Vessel realized its need,
for on either side of the cobbled path, a million beautiful flowers, were
dancing in the breeze.

WITH ME

He could stay in the Bahamas, if that is what He wants,
or He could sail the Caribbean, in a ninety-foot yacht.
He could dine in famous restaurants that serve fancy cuisine,
or create something new that has never yet been seen.

He could stroll across the stars, that He created one day,
but here by my side is where He would much rather stay.
He could make another planet or take a walk on the sea,
but He would rather spend all of His time here With Me.

He could make another river, a new mountain or two,
but He is more concerned, with what I'm going through.
When I'm having problems, He won't run and hide,
for when things are their worst, He is right here by my side.

He could paint another rainbow or an evening sunset,
anything to get His mind off my problems so He could relax and forget.
He could make a beautiful waterfall, a peaceful brook or stream,
but He would rather spend all of His time here With Me.

He could turn His back when I call His name,
and just go someplace quiet and secluded, forever to stay.
But He died on a cross, to show me that He cares,
and whenever I need Him, He is always right there.

He could spend His day floating high on a cloud,
surveying all He's created, and feeling ever so proud.
But instead of admiring all of His great feats,
He would rather go for a leisurely walk here With Me.

ROAD TO NOWHERE

I was on the Road to Nowhere, with no destination in my mind,
every turn I took was a dead end, to the left or to the right.
I wandered along aimlessly, with no vision in my sight;
So empty was my heart, thoughts were never given to my plight.
On the Road to Nowhere relationships were of no concern,
I never built bridges, instead every bridge I crossed, I burned.
Then I began to notice those around me, I wasn't so focused on myself,
I saw others full of happiness, even if they had no wealth.
To find the source of this happiness, I knew not where to begin,
for The Road to Nowhere only leads to frustrations that never seems to end.
Then one day I took a turn and saw a cross upon a church,
I stepped inside for just a moment, what could one moment possibly hurt.
In that moment I met Jesus, who died for me at Calvary,
now the road I'm walking, thank God, takes me to eternity.

CAN YOU SAVE ME

My time on earth was growing short, and I knew that I was lost,
so before it got much later, I would find someone to save me,
no matter what the cost.
I had no idea where to look as I hurried up the street,
but I thought I'd gotten lucky right off the bat, when Education was the first one I should meet.
He said, "I have all the answers! Is there a question you'd like to ask?"
Quickly I replied, "Can You Save Me, if it's not too great a task?"
With a puzzled look, he answered, "You've ask me the only thing I do not know,
I'm brilliant beyond belief, but I don't have a clue, about how to save your soul."

As I walked past a building, Science came walking out the door,
so I grabbed him by the arm, and ask the same question, I had asked before.
He said, "I mix things together, I split atoms, and make rockets fly,
but if you're asking me to make you eternal life, then you'll just have to die."
Then, across the street, I saw someone I trusted,
sitting on a park bench outside the bank.
I said, "Riches, Can You Save Me? You know, number one with me is always where you rank."
He answered, "I can buy you oil wells, real estate, and great big fancy yachts,
But, friend, I can't write a check big enough to buy you what you want."

Finally I had given up on being saved, it had been a hard and tiring search,
So I stopped and rested on a bench, in the shade of an old beat-up, rundown church.
As the sun set behind me, on the ground it cast the shadow of a cross,
and I heard a preacher's voice say, "Come to Jesus, He is the only one, who can save you if your lost."

FORGOTTEN

Like a child at a window that waits and watches anxiously,
His children watch for His return, knowing when He comes again, we will leave.
We look forward to the journey, when He comes to take His children home.
when we travel with the King of Kings, the One the grave could never hold.
But some say, "If He were coming, He would have come back by now."
I guess they've Forgotten Calvary and a crown of thorns that cut into His brow.
The cross is very beautiful when made into jewelry to wear,
but to His children, it is also a reminder of His love and just how much he cares.

Time moves so slowly, as we watch for Jesus to come back again,
but to the One who created time, only a short time has it been.
If you think He has Forgotten us or we're no longer part of His plans,
I'm sure, we are all He thinks about, each time He sees those scars in His hands.
Think of Mount Calvary, just picture that terrible sight,
in pain our savior bleeding, nailed to a cross there to die.
Think how much He loves us, just think what that love cost,
if you think He has Forgotten us, then you have Forgotten the cross.

MY NAME

If you should introduce me to some friends that we might meet,
I know they won't be awestruck, when they are introduced to me.
I'm sure they have never seen my face or even know my name,
since I'm not on a billboard sign or in some hall of fame.

I have never performed on Broadway or on some late night TV show,
nor do folks tune in from coast to coast to hear me on the radio.
So if people here don't know me, that doesn't wound my pride,
for the King of Kings knows My Name, He wrote it down in the book of life.

My names' never been on the silver screen, for a starring role I played,
and you won't see it on a big marquee or in the headlines every day.
I'm never ask for my autograph, and I'm not idolized,
but in the only place that matters, My Name is in bold type.

No, I'm not worldly famous, My Name is never up in lights,
but I know that Jesus knows me, I am why He came and died.
No, I'm not worldly famous, My Name isn't widely recognized,
but it is written down in big bold print, in God's great book of life.

SALVATION CRUISE

I've got my ticket in my hand, and I'm really feeling grand,
in spite of these ole worldly blues.
Because I'm headed to a place, where there's a smile on every face,
and there you never ever hear bad news.
Here the forecasts stay the same, clouds of burden, sorrow, and pain,
and here you hardly ever get good news.
The last good news I got was that all my sins were bought,
and I have a passport on that Salvation Cruise.

I got the cruise and the tour both free, from my friend at Calvary,
and He didn't charge me a single dime.
When I hear that trumpet blow, I'll know it's time to go,
and my Salvation Cruise could leave at any time.

There'll be so much to see, the tour will take an eternity,
and I'll be staying in a mansion with a tremendous view.
They say it is something to behold, walking on those streets of gold,
with friends and old loved ones that I once knew.
I'll be sailing in first class, in spite of my sinful past,
since Jesus died to give me life anew.
As we sail the crystal sea, then dock at the port of tranquility,
I'll thank my Lord and Savior for my Salvation Cruise.

DEATH

Death is full of sorrow and breaks our hearts in two,
but the time God calls a loved one home is not up to me or you.
God knows the time and hour from the moment our time begins,
and each breath we breathe is in His hands from the beginning to the end.
Tears will flow from broken hearts for those we dearly love,
but know their mission was complete and planned by God above.
He will fill the void in our hearts when our loved one we cannot touch,
as He sends the Holy Spirit to assure us that we're still loved.
So know Jesus defeated Death that day He walked out of the tomb,
and because of that victory, the one we lost has begun life anew.

EARTH

I've been here from the beginning, in my orbit here in space,
I saw God hang the sun and the moon, and put each star in its place.
I've been here from day one and I've seen it all,
from man living in caves to building skyscrapers tall.
I've watched him from the time he discovered fire, to inventing the wheel,
to surfing the internet;
from Cain slaying Abel with a stone, to killing one another with passenger jets.
I've felt nuclear bombs, floods, fires, and hurricane winds,
had dynamite and bulldozers cut me time and time again.
I remember when it rained forty days and nights,
and I remember a man who turned water into wine.
I'll never forget the time He walked on a stormy sea,
then, softly spoke to calm a ragging wind, to help His disciples believe.

But of all the things I remember the most since the beginning of time,
was the day they drove a cross into me, then hung Him there to die.
Now, I've had blood spilled on me many times before,
many times by accident, and thousands of times by weapons of war.
But His blood felt different that day, as it spilled down on me,
there was a power in it, a power like I'd never seen.
It caused the sun to darken and made me tremble and quake;
I realized then, this was the creator's son they had nailed to that stake.
For three days, He lay alone in my bowels dark and cold,
but then on the third day, from the dead he arose.

On the first day, the creator's words I did not understand,

when, as He made a mountain these words, He said, "Here I will sacrifice My son to save man."

Yes, I've seen it all from the time I was created on that first day,

from God breathing life into man, to putting death in its place.

From the garden of Eden, to his walk on the moon,

I've watched man turn from God, in what he calls, "Man's search for the truth."

The real truth, some men cannot understand,

Is the undying love that God has for man.

Though I am laden with oil, uranium, silver, and gold,

man is more valuable to God, than all the riches I hold.

Of all His great works, to God, man has always came first,

I should know! I've been here from the beginning, "I Am Earth."

IT'S CHRISTMAS

Shoppers scurry to and fro, what to give they just don't know,
they're searching for that special gift.
The gift must be the perfect size and most appealing to the eye,
it must be the very best, nothing less will do,
It's Christmas!

God looked down from up above, on the world He made and loves,
that night He gave the perfect gift.
In a manger small in size and unappealing to the eye,
God gave His son, nothing less would do.
It's Christmas!

Shoppers crowd into every store, pushed and shoved on every floor,
the gift requires this sacrifice and painstaking care.
Then wrapped up with a pretty bow, so that all who see will know,
how much love is in the perfect gift.
It's Christmas!

Jesus came from Heaven above, to be scourged, mocked, and shoved,
and sacrificed in brutal pain, to show how much God cares.
Then wrapped in ribbons of blood at Calvary, hanging on a cross for all to see,
just how much love is in the perfect gift.
It's Christmas!

HIGHWAY OF HOLINESS

I walked life's road of pebbles and stones,
and I fell so many times.
My garments carried its stain, my body bent from the pain,
of life's road and its long weary climb.
Alone I had to face Satan's beast that gave chase,
as I wandered in a dry barren land.
Then a friend I forgot, though I'm in His every thought,
said, "Reach out and take hold of my hand."

Now His blood shows the way; the way He paved for the saved,
and beneath His blood lies a safe highway home.
In spotless garments of white, I walk a road clean and bright,
and with Jesus, I am never alone.
No beasts roam up here, there is no sorrow only cheer,
as saints shout His name with joyfulness.
Soon I will dine at a feast with old loved ones I will meet,
who have traveled the Highway Of Holiness.

IT WAS LOVE

He could have called ten thousand angels and saved His life that day;
but He chose to stay and die for the sinful world He came to save.
Jesus could have said, "They're not worth it, it's just too great a cost."
but His love for us was greater, and love kept Him on the cross.
He could have stayed in heaven, turned His back, and walked away,
but on His back He carried our cross, with love in each step He made.

From the cross He said, "Forgive them" as teardrops filled His eyes,
it was a broken heart filled with love, not those nails that made Him cry.
It Was Love, not nails that held Him to that cross on Calvary,
It Was Love, not nails that killed Him, when He died for you and me.

KEYS

There lives a wicked jailer, in hell down below,
he uses sin to chain and bind us, and hopes to never let us go.
Each sin is like one small link, until he has a chain,
as we struggle to free ourselves, our strength we cannot regain.
For every chain there is a lock, and for every lock a key,
he wraps his chains around us, then locks them carefully.
When we're unable to break the chains, to the jailer we then plead,
but he only locks them tighter, then throws away the key.

From a baby in a manger, to a cross at Calvary,
God sent His son Jesus, to seize each and every key.
He battled Satan in the bowels of hell, for three days and nights without rest,
then Jesus seized the jailer's Keys by overcoming death.
When the chains of sin have you weighted down until you're on bended knee,
call on the name of Jesus, and He will come and set you free.
Jesus truly holds the Keys to life, for all eternity,
if you hold fast to the master, you hold the master key.

RUNNING WITH THE WIND

Soon, my spirit will be free to go where e're I please;
so I'll take a trip around the world and sail the seven seas.
I'll cross the mighty glaciers up Alaska way,
and run through the forest of Germany, before the end of day.
I'll shake the trees of autumn and float golden leaves into a stream,
as I go rushing up a canyon, beneath an eagle's wings.

Along the coast of Ireland, I'll make flowers dance upon the hills,
then make my way to Holland, to turn the farmer's magnificent windmills.
As I sweep across the great southwest, to climb the Rocky Mountains high,
fields of wheat will wave beneath me, as I roll clouds across the sky.
I will fill the sails of a vessel as it travels the ocean blue,
but as I do all these things, not once, will I forget the love I have for you.

I'll see all the things we talked about, and all you would love to see,
from the Golden Gate in Frisco Bay, to the streets of Gay Paree.
I'll see everything God has made with His two mighty hands,
and everything of interest, made by mortal man.
Don't think because I'm leaving, I won't pass this way again,
I'll come by most every day, to see just how you've been.
So when you're sitting quietly and the breeze kisses your soft skin,
just reach out and touch me, as I go Running with the Wind.

THE SEA OF FORGETFULNESS

Somewhere there is a sea, whose waters are dark and vast,
and in that sea, our sins are thrown if we only ask.
Its awesome waters are dark in color because of the sins it holds,
and when our sins are cast into it, they sink like a granite stone.

He needed a place to leave our faults, so they would not be seen again,
so into the deep, dark waters, God cast our every sin.
There they are forgotten as they sink into the great abyss,
and without this sea to drown my sins, eternity I would have missed.

Our savior goes to the waters' edge several times a day,
not to drink, or rest there, but to throw our sins away.
Once a sin has been thrown in it is forgotten for evermore,
for there aren't waves upon the sea, to wash it back to shore.

God prepared a mansion for me, it is built along golden streets,
and I hope a window will have a view, of that vast dark sea.
Though it is not beautiful, like the sea of tranquility,
at the bottom of The Sea of Forgetfulness lies my every inequity.

MY RAGGED OLD TENT

I look back into the distance at the places I have been,
as I continue on my journey with My Ragged Old Tent.
I remember every valley; some very dark and deep,
all the mountains I had to climb that were rocky and so very steep.
I can see that dry, barren desert, where I nearly died of thirst,
but I realize now, it could have all been much worse.

It's been a long hard journey, across an unforgiving land,
and I would have never made it without my Father's plan.
But I trusted in His word, and used it as my guide,
when I happened to take the wrong road or my way I could not find.
Father said as He left, "A mansion awaits at your journeys end,
but until you reach your destination, travel with this tent."

Now there on the horizon, is the landmark He said I'd see,
a cross, standing high on a mountain, called Calvary.
Just beyond that mountain lies a river where I will camp tonight;
then rise up early in the morning and cross over at first light.
When Father hears that my journey is over, and I have arrived,
with outstretched arms He'll greet me, when He calls me to the other side.

This will be the last night that I'll have any need for it here;
for just across the river, the voices of old loved ones, sound so very near.
Though it withstood the winds, the rain, and the torment of life's storms,
I now have no use for this old tent anymore.
So here by this peaceful river where a new life begins,
is the place I will be leaving, My Ragged Old Tent.

THE MAN FROM THE BOX

Life was getting to me, I just had to get away,
if just for a few minutes, on this peculiar day.
I knew I would not be missed, and half a day was not too much to steal,
so I drove by my house and picked up favorite rod and reel.
I just started driving until I came to a stream where I saw a secluded place.
Here, I hoped I could clear my mind and get bad thoughts replaced.

A path led me to the bank of the stream, and there sat an empty wooden chair,
I thought, how lucky I was that someone forgot it, and left it setting there.
After putting a lure on my line, I cast it out beside a big brush pile;
then sat down in the chair to relax, if just for a little for a while.
It was really peaceful here, and I didn't care if I got a bite,
just nice to sit and watch the squirrels play, and listen to the birds in flight.

Suddenly, something sent cold chills up and down my spine,
when I heard something and saw a movement out of the corner of my eye.
"Having any luck?" a voice ask.
"Don't care if I catch a thing," I answered back.
He was a breaded man, with suntanned skin and soft brown eyes.
He said, "Sorry, friend, I did not mean to catch you by surprise."

I asked, "Where did you come from?" as I looked at the trees and rocks.
He pointed at a grove of trees, and there I saw a canvas-covered cardboard box.
"Cast your line on the other side of that brush pile,
and you will catch a big catfish," He said, with a knowing smile.

To my surprise, my lure had barely hit the water when I got a strike,
and sure enough, I caught a big catfish, with a lot of fight.

"Nothing like going fishing to help clear your mind!" he said,
I know this world will torment a man and get inside his head.
I said, "I worry about my job, and finances, and decisions I've made,
I want the best for my family, and I don't want them to know, that I'm afraid.
Seems like a new problem hits me every time I turn around,
You're right old man, when you say this world can beat a person down."

He said, "If you are troubled, and life is causing you to have fear and doubt,
you know, there is someone you can talk to, who is always glad to help you out.
His name is Jesus, and He is concerned with what you're going through,
He is always there to hear your problems and He truly cares for you.
So don't think you're in this by yourself, to take the world on alone,
He is eager to help see you through, and wants to shoulder your heavy load."

We talked for more than an hour, The Man from the Box and me,
and He had exceptional wisdom, like no one I'd ever seen.
I handed Him the fish I caught and said, "This should make a meal."
As I started back to my car, I realized I had forgotten my rod and reel.
When I turned around, where I had been, there stood a doe and her baby fawn,
I looked in the trees where I'd seen the box, and it and the man were gone.

As I picked up my rod and reel, I touch the arm of the wooden chair,
and I felt a peace like never before, as I breathed in the cool, clean air.
As I drove back to the city with my new frame of mind,
I couldn't wait to get back home to the kids and embrace my beautiful wife.
I thought what a wonderful day this has been, though it did seem rather odd;
I wondered, did I fall asleep in that chair, or had I been fishing with God.

HE LEFT THE LIGHT ON

God gave His Son Jesus to save us from sin,
and He is the light that never grows dim.
He will light up your life like when night meets the dawn,
God is the power, and He Left the Light On.

God sent a light, so a dark world might see,
and He still shows the way, for those who believe.
He is the way, the truth, and the light,
and He will forever shine brightly, in day or the night.

If your soul is like a cottage where no one lives anymore,
and you feel beaten down, weary, and worn;
If you stand in the darkness thinking all hope is gone,
don't worry my friend He Left the Light On.

If you think He's forgotten or He won't know who you are,
or you think You have missed Him since you've journeyed so very far.
When you turn back for home, you will know He hasn't gone,
for you will see a glow in a window, and know He Left the Light On.

WHAT WOULD HAVE BEEN

Without Jesus, I would walk in loneliness,
without His love, there would be emptiness.
Without Calvary, I would have no place to take my sins,
without Jesus, think What Would Have Been.

Without Jesus, the world would have no guide,
without His love, hope would be dark as night.
Without Calvary, the grave would be the end,
without Jesus, think what would have been.

Without Jesus, there would be no hope for me,
without out His love, I would have no inner peace.
Without Calvary, my soul He could not win,
without Jesus, think What Would Have Been.

Without Jesus, without His love, without Calvary,
 What Would Have Been?

LEAN ON THE CROSS

I've been walking all day, I've came a long, long way,
and my steps have grown weary and weak.
But there's the hill up ahead, where my dear savior bled,
and it's the door step to the home that I seek.
I thank God for this climb, to the victory that's mine,
for without this old hill, I would be lost.
Now, as my breath leaves my chest, I see a good place to rest,
I'll just lean on that old rugged cross.

Now when I see that old hill, my heart is so thrilled,
for I know once again I've found my way.
It's a landmark for me, and from its top I can see,
my new home where I forever will stay.
Between this world and glory land, an old mountain still stands,
and they call that old hill Calvary.
For a while I will stop and rest at the top,
I'll just Lean on the Cross, where Jesus saved me.

WATER ON THE ROCKS

Ole' Moses led God's people, on a forty-year long trip,
they wondered in the desert, with no water there to sip.
God was always faithful, he gave them quail and manna every day,
He met their needs and gave them strength as they travel on their way.
God told Moses, "Speak to a rock, and it would spew water out to drink,"
but all the gripping by the people, had Moses's temper on the brink.
So in anger Moses struck the stone, not once, but once again,
but God was loyal to His word, and from the rock poured water from within.

Now Samson was a mighty man with hair way down past his shoulders,
but without the strength God gave him, he would have been a lot less bolder.
Yes, Samson was the strongest man that ever walked upon our planet,
but without God inside him, he couldn't wreck that temple made of granite.
But before he tore that temple down, he made an army look like silly fools,
when he slew them one and all, with the jawbone of a cousin to a mule.
Samson had worked up a terrible thirst, after such a great and awesome feat,
so God cracked a rock, and out came rushing water, so Samson got a drink.

As we take our walk down life's road, the journey can be a long and tiring trip,
with pits that make us stumble and mountains where we might slip.
Sometimes we'll feel deserted and think we're in the darkness all alone,
we'll feel weak and weary and think we've sunk as far as we can go.
But when our faith is tired and thirsty and lying on the jagged rocks,
that's when God will quench our thirst, with Water on the Rocks.

THE ADVOCATE

As I sat in the witness box trembling and scared,
the prosecutor rose, then looked at me and glared.
He called out each sin I had committed in life,
and through a crooked smile, he chuckled with sheer delight.
There was fire in his eyes and smoke on his breath,
as he began to poke his finger into my chest.

He raised a clenched fist as he began to yell,
and I was sure that forever, I would burn in hell.
He said, "You're the scum of the earth, I recommend death for your sins,"
as he loudly, reminded me of all my inequities again.
"How do you plea?" He asked, as violently he began waving his arms,
I dropped my head and sadly answered, "Guilty as charged."

He yelled, "Take him away, the prosecution rests,
everyone here heard the defendant confess."
Then above the intimidating courtroom noise,
I heard a strong yet gentle, confident voice.
My hope was renewed when the gentle voice said,
"I came here to save this man, for him there will be no death."

Then, from the crowd stepped a man with a large book in one hand,
I figured Him to be a highly educated Yale or Harvard man.
I knew His fee would be expensive and I could not pay,

I thought, I might as well start serving my sentence today.
When He opened the book and turned to a certain page,
He said, "Here is this man's name, and here it will stay."

With two nailed scarred hands, He raised the book up high,
then He declared, "In my hands, I hold the book of life."
He said, "This man shall live forever, because he believes in me,
and from the evil prosecutor, he will be set free."
What He said next caused a hush to fall over the rowdy court room,
He said, "I erased his sins, when I died on the cross, then rose from the tomb."

NO TIME

I sat outside the office of an executive I hoped to see,
but after waiting for an hour, I was told, "He had No Time for me."
So disappointed, I left his office and went across the street,
in hopes another CEO might at least acknowledge me.
But a lady sitting behind a desk told me, "Have a seat,
while I make an appointment for you to see him sometime next week."
Then she gave me his card, and as she showed me to the door,
she said, "I squeezed you in for three minutes next Thursday,
at fifteen minutes after four."

As I left the building, a man stepped from a chauffeured limousine,
but I was told by his bodyguard, "This man only speaks to people with prestige."
I decided to head on home, now that my feelings had really been hurt,
when I heard bells ring out somewhere from a distance church.
As I listened to the bells ring, and as they began to chime,
I said to myself, "Thank you, Jesus, for giving me your time."
I thought how Jesus died for me and how His blood spilled to the ground,
as I kept walking toward those bells and their beautiful ringing sound.

I thought, though I'm not important to these high and mighty men,
I am important enough to Jesus, that He came and died for all my sins.
He did not make me set in a waiting room, staring at the walls,
while He set with His feet upon His desk, talking on a conference call.

Though He must get a thousand calls every minute or so,
not once have I gotten a recording and never have I been put on hold.
When I ask for His help, He listens intently,
and never ask the question, "What in turn is it, that you can do for me?"

Though the rich and famous have no time for me,
I can spend all the time I want with the greatest man in all eternity.
If the high and mighty are not careful, where their values have been put,
they could be waiting outside the pearly gates, with the shoe on the other foot.
For when they announce to Saint Peter, that they have arrived,
Saint Peter may just tell them, "You missed you appointment for Salvation,
and now for you, He has No Time."

HE BORROWED A DONKEY

No earthly riches did this king own,
though He came from a city, He built with jasper and gold.
He could have worn precious rubies, fine emeralds, and gowns,
and this King knew He would die, wearing thorns for a crown.
This King owned no chariots in which to ride,
He just walked in sandals, as He healed the blind.

He Borrowed a Donkey, to ride into town,
knowing when He did, His blood would spill to the ground.
This King gave His life and never questioned the cost,
That day, when He borrowed my place on the cross.

He borrowed a penny, His words to explain,
when they tried to tempt Him, with what Caesar should gain.
He borrowed two small fish and five loaves of bread,
then on a mountain five thousand He fed.
This king owned no castles, no vast real estate,
in fact when they killed Him, He borrowed a grave.
When this king returns, He will claim all the water and land,
everything He created with His own two hands.

He Borrowed a Donkey to ride into town,
knowing when He did, His blood would spill to the ground.
This King gave His life and never questioned the cost,
that day, when He borrowed my place on the cross.

RED CARPET

As I walked through the gate toward the mansion ahead,
I hoped for a good meal, but would settle for dry bread.
I've asked for handouts at nice places like this before,
and they send you 'round back, when they see that you're poor.
But I would ask at the front, for food in a small sack,
and a cool drink of water, slipped through a window 'round back.

When I rang the bell at the door, the sound was so grand,
a great trumpet sound, that shook the whole land.
Then, the door opened, and there stood a man,
who greeted me with a smile, and two badly scarred hands.
I said, "I've came along way down a hard dirty path,
so I beg of you, sir, a meal and warm bath."
I was confused when He said, "Come on in,
I know of you journey, for I was with you, my friend."

When I shook His scarred hand, my body glowed,
and my old garments became new and whiter than snow.
Then, He took me inside to a banquet to eat,
He really rolled out the Red Carpet for me.
I said, "I can't pay, are there chores I can do,
to show my thanks and appreciation to you?"
He smiled and answered, "Don't worry about chores,
for you owe me nothing, and this mansion, it's yours."

I was overwhelmed, to say the least,

and my mind was racing, as I sat down to feast.

I could not remember where I knew this man from,

but the more I thought, recollection began to come.

Then my mind clicked, and I recognized His face,

and as my thoughts came together, I remembered the place.

He was Jesus! The man who died on the cross at mount Calvary,

the place, where with His blood, He first, rolled out the Red Carpet for me.

MY GUARDIAN

My soul is defenseless and weak like a lamb,
as it grazes in a meadow, surrounded by a harsh and wicked land.
A wolf lurks in the shadows stalking my every move,
waiting to attack me, so my soul it can consume.

My Guardian is a lion, watching His flock both night and day,
ever watchful for the wolf who seeks lost souls that go astray.
When the wolf springs forth against me, the lion hears my plea;
His power is quick and mighty and causes the wolf to flee.

As daylight turns to dusk and then turns into night,
the wolf can be heard in the darkness, taking lost souls with all his might.
But I fear not when shadows fall across the wicked land,
for when darkness comes, My Guardian lies down beside His precious lamb.

THE BOOK THAT SAYS IT ALL

As I stepped inside the bookstore, I saw books from wall to wall,
so I knew it should not be too difficult, to find The Book That Says It All.
I started down the center aisle, searching every shelf;
finding books on everything from making bombs to caring for your health.
There were books about world wars, and dinosaurs, and every kind of fish,
books on how to raise your children and how to prepare a gourmet dish.
Books about violent storms, written by meteorologists explaining why it rains,
medical books by doctors, diagnosing every ache and pain.
Rows of books about love and romance and murder mysteries of all kinds,
books written in different languages, and books written for the blind.
Books about sailing ships, all our presidents, and books about the law;
by now it was half past noon, and I had not yet found The Book That Says It All.

Some books were thick while some were thin, and some weighed several pounds,
some used plain common words, while some used words I can't pronounce.
The lights came on before I noticed that darkness had began fall,
but that's when I saw a shelf with one small book in the nook of an offset wall.
Just for fun, I opened up the little book because I knew there was not a way,
for the book just had the front and back covers, and just one single page.
On that page, one word explained why rivers flow and the stars shine up above,
it told about the greatest battle ever won, and about the world's greatest love.
That word told how to calm a violent storm and how to really make it rain;
it told about The Great Physician who can heal the sick, the blind, or lame.
All that matters was consumed in that one word written in italics bold and tall,
that one word was Jesus! In The Book That Says It All.

THREE RUSTY NAILS

As Three Rusty Nails lay on a dirty shelf one began to speak,
"Have our lives been wasted here, or really, is it just me?"
"It's not just you," another replied, "I feel the same myself;
I've often wondered why I was made if only to rust away on a dirty shelf."

Then the third nail spoke and said, "I agree, this was not my life's ambition,
I dreamed of holding the shingle over the door of the world's best physician.
A physician so great He could heal anyone, and take away their pain;
one who could heal the blind or deaf, or even heal the lame."

As footsteps moved toward the shelf, the first nail spoke again.
"I wanted to support the main beam of a church, one pure and free of sin,"
Once again, the second nail spoke and said, "Please don't laugh at me,
but all I wanted to be was the hook on a wall, that held the robe of a king
of high royalty.

Then, as a Roman soldier took the three nails from the shelf he said,
"Use these to nail Jesus to the cross and put these thorns upon his head."
One of the nails said, "Did you hear that? We're being used to kill a man.
All of our dreams might have came true, if placed in a carpenter's hands."

THE STEWARD

I knew I should be busy, planting crops to raise and reap,
so my silos would be filled with grain and golden wheat.
But it was too soon, I thought, for the Master to come,
to look over His crops and see the work I'd done.

So I would put the work off, for yet another day,
and just rest 'neath a tree and enjoy the shade.
For the day was young, and I was not concerned,
about harvest time, and earth unturned.

But the Master did come, and He walked the hard ground,
and when in my silos no grain could be found.
He said, "I gave you land to till and seed to sow,
why is it then, my Steward, that no crops have been grown?"

As we looked upon my silos bare,
the Master asked, "Do you really care?"
As He left, He said, "Soon I'll return,
to look over the harvest, and see what wage you've earned."

The sun was high when I put my hand on the plow,
and with a sack of seed on my shoulder, I had to hurry now.
But when the sun set at the end of my day,
a crop was now growing in fields that where once was hard clay.

When I saw fields of wheat swaying in the gentle breeze,
my heart was thrilled and my mind was at ease.
When I knew my silos would no longer stand bare,
I lifted my voice to the heavens and said, "Yes, Master, I care."

A HAMMER AND THOSE NAILS

I've seen many pretty paintings of Jesus on the cross,
and to say just what they mean to me, my words are at a loss.
Why God would send His Son for me, then have Him die in pain,
is a love so blind and great, my simple words cannot explain.
As it stands there on a distant hill, in silence all alone,
an ole' bloodstained cross keeps speaking volumes to my soul.
A sound has echoed throughout the years, of a love that never fails,
it is the ringing of a hammer, driving in those rusty nails.
When they nailed Jesus to that cross, God's love did prevail,
and nothing rings love more clearly, than A Hammer and Those Nails.

We show our love with kisses, and the words, "I love you, dear,"
or with a lovely postcard that says, "Miss you, wish you were here."
We embrace our loved ones in our arms, whenever they are near,
write poetry and songs of love, that for a short while they will hear.
As we should, we show our love, with many different things.
We say, "I love you!" with bouquets of flowers, cards, and diamond rings.
But the sound of love that day at Calvary was a different kind of ring;
and it gave us a song of love, that forever we will sing.
When they nailed Jesus to that cross, God's love did prevail,
and nothing says love better than, A Hammer and Those Nails.

GUILTY

Guilty I stood before Him,
knowing He knew my every sin.
Too late, I realized there was no need for all my feeble plans,
for my destiny now lay in his precious, nail-scarred hands.
I planned on great accomplishments, not caring about the price,
but somewhere I lost my way and had left Him out of my life.
The world had consumed me, a fool I had been,
weak and helpless, on His word I now had to depend.
I read somewhere, He came to save me, and not judge what I had done,
that all my sins were cast into the sea of forgiveness, each and every one.
A voice asked the question, "How is it that you plea?"
I answered, "Guilty!" And the voice said, "Why Guilty, since I set you free?"
Then I heard Him say, "Raise your head, and look into my eyes,"
and there, I saw a love so great, that for me He came and died.
He said, "I took away all your sins that day at Calvary,
so don't let Satan tell you that you're Guilty, for I have set you set free."

THE PITCHER

The rival mocked and jeered, as I stood there on the mound,
and on my sleeve, I wiped my brow, as my sweat dripped to the ground.
I was winning and going strong in the early part of the game,
my curve was sharp and nasty, and my fast ball was a flame.
I had shut the rival and his teammates out, they had not a single hit,
and though it was getting late and I was tired, I did not want to quit.
But my rival knew I was tiring, so he kept bringing on the fight,
he knew my fastball was slowing down, and my curve had lost its bite.
My rival's team of demons were now picking me apart,
with line drives here and base hits there, I was beginning to lose heart.
The sun had started going down, and my spikes were heavy on my feet,
and though I had pitched my very best, I began to feel defeat.

But then, my rival heard a sound that dulled his laughter quite a bit;
it was the power of a blazing fastball, slapping in a catcher's mitt.
The sound came from my bull pen where my big reliever was warming up,
and now it was my rival, whose hopes were suddenly in the dump.
From the bull pen the sound got louder, like a hammer driving nails,
with my reliever ready to save me, my rival knew that I'd prevail.
I was very tired and weary, I had gone as far as I could go,
so I motioned to the bull pen, for my savior to bring the victory home.
My rival was not aware, but very early in the game I knew that I would win,
for I had that weapon in my bull pen on whom I could depend.
"You did fine," my Savior said, as I placed the ball in His nail-scarred hand,
and as I ducked into the dugout, the cheers were loud and grand.

GOD'S GREATNESS

As I stand here on this hillside, overlooking the valley down below,
I see flowers dancing in the mist, beneath a beautiful rainbow.

An eagle soars high overhead above a gentle stream,
as beams of sun light pierce the haze, so all of His beauty can be seen.

An oak tree standing beside the stream, puts His awesome strength on display;
and as the sun sets in the distance the colors take your breath away.

A doe and her fawn step from the safety of the trees,
and I see a cautious beauty in her eyes, as she stares back at me.

The doe stays alert and ready as her baby jumps, runs, and plays.
He's not showing off His work, it's just God's Greatness there on display.

WITH BOTH HANDS

You say, "You are giving up, because your spirit is down,
you just get tired of fighting when Satan comes around."
Friend, wipe away those tear drops, hope has been renewed,
for the battles you keep fighting, our Father fought and won for you.
God told Satan, "I fear thee not, though you torment, kill, and maim;
to defeat you for my children, I'll let you kill me, then I'll rise up from the grave.
I will meet you at Golgotha, as part of my salvation plan,
and for you to have a fighting chance, drive these nails into my hands."

Satan thought he had won the battle, when they met at Calvary,
where a bloodstained line was drawn, and they fought for you and me.
Satan was sure he had won the fight, when that spear pierced our Father's side,
but then he felt the earth quake and watched the sun turn dark as night.
Satan simply bowed his head, for he had fought his fight and lost,
that day our Father defeated him, With Both Hands nailed to a cross.

So when Satan comes against you with a new attack,
and claims he can defeat you with one arm tied to his back.
You don't have to raise your voice, just whisper Calvary,
tell him you are a child of God, then watch ole' Satan flee.
Satan knew he was defeated, when he fought his fight and lost,
that day our Father defeated him, With Both Hands nailed to a cross.

THE MAN FROM THE SHORE

We looked out at the water, as we stood there on dry land,
and when He pointed toward the horizon, I noticed an ugly scar on His hand.
He said, "It is calm right now, but it can get real mean,
I would love to be your pilot, I have a world of experience out there on the sea."
I said, "Thanks a lot, but no thanks just the same."
He replied, "If you ever change your mind, just call out Jesus, that's my name."

I raised anchor and hoisted the sail,
feeling ever so confident, that I could not fail.
The sea was smooth, and the breeze was kind,
not a worry in the world crossed my mind.
I was splitting the glass-smooth waters going full bore,
very proud of myself, for not bringing The Man from the Shore.

My sail was full as the breeze picked up,
then the sea began to swell, as waves started, causing my vessel to bump.
In the distance, thunderstorms rumbled as the wind gained force;
and my hands trembled on the wheel, as desperately I tried to stay on course.
When lightning ripped across the pitch-black sky,
it took my confidence with it, for I was now mortally terrified.

Now I began to lose hope as I lost control, and when waves slapped me down,
with no one to help me I knew I would soon drown.
With the bow high in the air and being thrown all about,

I knew now I was sinking; there was no doubt.

As I fought to hang on and not be thrown overboard,

I remembered the words spoken by The Man from the Shore.

I was sure it was too late, but I would try just the same,

so in the midst of the storm, I whispered, "Jesus!" I think that was His name.

Dazed, I looked up, as I lay flat on my back, down on the floor,

and to my surprise, there at the wheel, stood The Man from the Shore.

With His scarred hands firmly on the wheel, He swung the bow back around.

Then He spoke, "Peace, be still," and the winds died, and the sea calmed down.

I asked, "Where did you come from?" As I rose from my knees.

He answered, "I was walking right behind you, out there on the sea."

TODAY

The sands of time speed through the hourglass as I worry myself down to the core;
Instead of thinking more about others and leaving my problems to the Lord.

I'm sure He smiles a little bit as I prepare the perfect plan,
While thinking I can handle this, and not placing it
In His hands.

If I'd not worry and rush ahead, He would give me each victory.
He would give me more than I deserve and all
I really need.

Still I try to help God out, but I only get in
His way,
as I find Today is now tomorrow, that I worried about yesterday.

EXIT SIGNS

Everything was new and shiny when I first started out.
I was so excited to get started, I did not think about the route.
I burned a little rubber as I quickly got things in gear,
I didn't look where I was going, heading down the road without a fear.
The top was down, the RPMs were up I was really flying low;
when all of a sudden, I had to stop, I had come to a fork there in the road.

One sign pointed to Heaven, but the road was straight, with not much room;
so I went left down the broad way, it was wide and looked really smooth.
I was cruising in the fast lane with one hand upon the wheel,
Thinking, man, I'm glad I took this road, this is really a real good deal.
Then I saw another exit sign that read, "To Heaven exit here,"
but I raced on toward neon lights, that advertised wine and ice-cold beer.

The broad way kept getting wider, with flashing lights and signs every mile,
with promises of success and happiness, that really made me smile.
I kept the pedal to the metal, hoping I wouldn't get there last,
I didn't know where I was going, but I was going to get there fast.

My tires were making music on the broad way, they sang a happy song,
as I roared past another heaven exit sign; thinking nothing could go wrong.
Then suddenly, the lights went out on the broad way, there was darkness all around,
I couldn't see where I was going and drove into a pit that went straight down,
Now, I rust here in ruins; in a pile with others who have lost their shine.
Too late, I wish I would have followed those Heaven Exit Signs.

ALL OUTDOORS

As I looked out from a mountain, I thought, how big God must be,
to create everything, as far as my eyes can see.
From rivers and canyons, to great mountains tall,
how big God must be, to have created it all.
He said, "Let there be heavens, and let there be land,"
then He created it all, with the wave of His hand.
He can stand on the ocean, reach out and touch every shore,
for God is much bigger than All Outdoors.

I need not worry when problems come blowing my way; for my God can
calm the wind and turn night into day.
There is not a problem too big or a heartache too small,
as big as God is, He hears my faintest call.
There's no way to measure how big God must be,
for He can dip down one hand and empty the sea.
He can stand on the ocean, reach out and touch every shore,
for God is much bigger than All Outdoors.

KING OF THE HILL

They went up on a hill to do battle one day,
winner take all, all our souls were at stake.
Satan took all his army and every demon he had,
while Jesus took a cross, and His two bare hands.
He could have ran from the conflict, choosing not to fight;
knowing full well, on that hill, was where He would die.
When both powers collided, and His blood spilled,
when Jesus said, "It is finished," He was King of the Hill.

Satan knew the importance, he spared no cost,
but he was beaten by Jesus, with an old rugged cross.
Jesus rose from the dead, and He's living still,
and our souls were saved that day, by the King of the Hill.
Yes, a battle was raging for you and me,
when they fought on that hill that's called Calvary.
Jesus died on the cross, knowing that was God's will,
He was victorious, He is King of the Hill.

IN THE TWINKLING OF AN EYE

In The Twinkling of an Eye, we'll be nine miles in the sky,
when our dear lord raptures you and me.
When Jesus steps out on a cloud, and Gabriel blows his trumpet loud,
to call us to our heavenly home to live for eternity.
There won't be time to pack, there will be no looking back,
as we meet old loved ones in the air.
First, graves will open wide as sleeping saints rise up in heavenly flight;
and we rejoin them in that place, where there's no worry not a care.

In The Twinkling of an Eye, we'll not have time for goodbye,
when Jesus comes to claim His chosen few.
If He is not your Lord and King, you won't hear the angels sing;
and I wouldn't want to be left here in your shoes.
His coming will be quick, before a clock can tick,
and surely it could be this very night.
Friend don't tarry very long, heed the message in those old gospel songs,
take Jesus as your savior, now's the time.

In The Twinkling of an Eye, He will split the eastern sky,
as all of God's power is revealed.
There is no more time to waste, friend, please don't hesitate,
for when He comes our fate forever, will be sealed.
He has left us many signs, when He will come for His heavenly bride,
and the signs say the time is very near.
He could come back day or night, only God knows the exact time;
but if He is your savior, you don't have a thing to fear.

MY FRIEND

I met this friend sometime ago when I was just a child.
He has stayed beside me ever since, every step of every mile.
Though I've asked His forgiveness more times than I can count;
He is right there when I need Him, in His love there in no doubt.
My Friend was showing His love for me before we ever met;
like the time He came and died for me I never will forget, When they placed
Him in the tomb for me, He rose again,
because of My Friend, the grave is not the end.

Though I often stumble and every time I fall,
My Friend is there when I reach out, all I have to do is call.
He is there in the sunshine, He is there in the rain;
When my heart is feeling light or when it's filled with pain.
He has a place prepared for me when this world ends,
that's how I know He loves me and still wants me for His friend.
But I'm not worthy to go there on my own,
only through My Friend may I call heaven home.

Oh! I'm so glad Jesus is My Friend,
He is always there to comfort me, on that I can depend.
Fair-weather friends come and go according to my needs,
but Jesus is a friend who is there at my faintest plea.
He came and died on the cross for my every sin.
Because of My Friend, I will live again.
I'm so glad, Jesus is My Friend!